Star
in the
Forest

Star
in the
Forest

LAURA RESAU

SCHOLASTIC INC.

ISBN 978-0-545-52316-5

Text copyright © 2010 by Laura Resau.
Cover art and interior illustrations copyright © 2010 by Gary Blythe.
All rights reserved. Published by Scholastic Inc., 557 Broadway, New York, NY 10012,
by arrangement with Yearling, an imprint of Random House Children's Books,
a division of Random House, Inc. SCHOLASTIC and associated logos
are trademarks and/or registered trademarks of Scholastic Inc.

12 11 10 9 8 7 6 5 4 3 2 1   13 14 15 16 17 18/0

Printed in the U.S.A.   40

First Scholastic printing, January 2013

Para mis queridos amigos Zitlally, Cuauhtemoc,
Alejandro, y Erick . . . y todos los niños que
están separados de sus familias por fronteras

For my good friends Zitlally, Cuauhtemoc,
Alejandro, and Erick . . . and all children who
are separated from their families by borders

Moquetzalizquixochintzetzeloa in icniuhyotl.

La amistad es lluvia de flores preciosas.

Friendship is a shower of precious flowers.

— AYOCUAN CUETZPALTZIN
fifteenth-century Aztec poet
from the region of Puebla, Mexico

Acknowledgments

This book would not exist without inspiration from Gloria Garcia Díaz—a talented writer and close friend—and her lovely nieces Frida and Karla. *Gracias*, Gloria, for the conversations that led to this book, and for your enthusiastic feedback on the manuscript! I'm grateful to my friend Javier and his family for sharing Nahuatl expertise, as well as tales of magical forests, stars, and mushroom hunting. Thanks, also, to my ESL students, who teach me about the many facets of life as an immigrant.

Heaps of gratitude go to Old Town Writing Group's Carrie, Leslie, Sarah, Katers, and Lauren—who fill my writing life with laughter and fabulous critiques.

Gracias to my bilingual educator friends Michelle, Paul, Martha, and Samara for their wonderful suggestions, and to the immigration lawyer Kim Salinas for vividly explaining deportation procedures. My extraordinary editor, Stephanie Lane Elliott, and her assistant, Krista Vitola, deepened this book with their creative insights. With each new book, I feel luckier to be working with the amazing people at Random House Children's Books and with my magnificent agent, Erin Murphy.

As always, my mom, Chris, gave me brilliant advice on every single draft of this book. She's been encouraging my storytelling from the time I was a four-year-old chattering about butter ice-skating across a hot pan. My dad, Jim, has shown me the value of friendships between people of different cultures, and has always encouraged my travels. I'm grateful to my toddler son, Bran, for making me laugh and lick sunshine and love with all my heart. And the biggest thank-you of all goes to Ian, who (despite nagging about the dishes that pile up in the sink while I write) has made my life a sweet soul dream.

PART ONE

Star

· 1 ·

There is a forest behind my trailer, through the weeds and under the gate and across the trickly, oily ditch. It is a forest of very, very old car parts, heaps of rusted metal, spotted orangey brown, with rainbow layers of fading paint, and leaves and vines poking and twisting through the holes. Birds and snakes and bugs sometimes peek out from the pipes and hubcaps. My neighborhood is called

3

Forest View Mobile Home Park. I think this must be the forest they're talking about.

On the day Papá was deported, that's where I went.

The police had pulled him over a week earlier, and while he was in jail, Mamá was on her cell phone all the time.

Deportado, deportado, deportado, she said, in a hushed, dangerous voice.

Deportado, she said to my aunts Rosa and Virginia and María.

Deportado, she said over the phone to Uncle Luciano in Mexico.

Deportado meant Papá would be sent back to Mexico, and it would be very, very hard for him to come back.

The day before he was deported, I saw Papá at the jail. He stared at me through the scratchy plastic divider. The phone shook in his hand. He said, "Goodbye, Zitlally." Then he whispered, "*Ni-mitz nequi.*" I love you.

He looked strange in the blue jumpsuit, and even stranger because he was crying, right there in front of the other prisoners and their families and the guards. But my tears stayed hidden under a stone inside a cave inside me. I worried that Papá thought I wasn't sad because my face was dry when I said goodbye.

The next day, alone in the car part forest, I felt tears pushing out like a geyser.

My name is Zitlally. *Estrella.* Star. That's what it means in Nahuatl. Nahuatl is what Papá speaks to me in secret, even though I don't understand. It is a soft language full of *shhhhs* and perfect for whispering at night. I used to think it was the language of the stars, what they whispered to each other. This year during the Mexico unit in school, I found out it was the language of the Aztecs. The Aztecs are supposed to be all dead. Maybe they're the ones whispering. I didn't tell anyone that their words aren't dead. I know because Papá speaks them. Because he named me one. Because I hear the stars whispering. *Shhhh.*

The day after Papá was *deportado*, Mamá was on the phone saying *deportado, deportado* and crying and Reina was watching a murder movie on TV and Dalia was hanging out with her friends at the edge of the park that no kids are allowed to go to because of the broken glass and needles. Usually Mamá would frown and Papá would say that Dalia couldn't hang out with them and that Reina couldn't watch murder movies, but now that Mamá was always on the phone, saying *deportado, deportado*, she didn't notice much.

I brought my math worksheets outside and sat on the ripped Astroturf porch, leaning against the tin side of our trailer. I shivered and wished I'd brought a sweater. It was a little cold because it was April.

Fractions. Four-fifths. The fraction of my family here. Papá used to look over my shoulder as I did math homework and help me. He didn't do problems the way Mr. Martin did on the board.

He had his own system. He was a framer and always had to cut wood perfectly, down to the exact one-eighth of an inch, and not waste any wood. He was a master of fractions.

Something crashed, something glass. It came from next door. Then came a waterfall of bashing and breaking and yelling. It was that girl, Crystal's, mom and her mom's boyfriend.

I never talked to Crystal at school.

My best friend, Morgan, said that Crystal shopped at garage sales.

My second-best friend, Emma, said she had poor dental hygiene and chronic halitosis.

And my third-best friend, Olivia, said she used to pee in her pants in first grade.

Since they were my best friends forever, I knew where my loyalty was. When Crystal tried to talk to me at the bus stop, I just shrugged and smiled with no teeth and looked away.

In the two years we'd been friends, Emma and Morgan and Olivia were always inviting me to go ice-skating or to the mall or to the movies or something. It was hard work being their friend. It made me feel like a nervous squirrel, always with my eyes big and my ears perked up.

I had to watch their clothes to know what to wear. Watch their hair to know how to do mine. Watch how they stood and sat and walked so I could do the same. I had to listen to which words they used so I could use them, too. Listen to how their voices went up at the end of a sentence so I could make mine an echo.

There's a reason squirrels do dumb things like run in front of cars. They're all muddled up from so much watching and listening.

In the weeks after Papá was deported, sometimes I accidentally wore the same pair of jeans two days in a row. Sometimes I didn't bother brushing my hair in the morning. When Morgan told jokes, sometimes I forgot to laugh. I was usually staring at a thin line of dirt under my fingernail. Or the tiny scar on my knuckle. Or a raggedy cuticle.

When Olivia asked me to the indoor pool, and Emma asked me to sleep over, I mumbled excuses. At school, no one wanted me in their reading group anymore. I stared at my hands instead of talking. My words were starting to disappear, the way the last bits of snow were melting into mud.

One day, Emma invited me to ride bikes in the park—not our broken-glass park—they never came to my neighborhood—but the nice park by her house.

"I can't," I said.

"Why not?"

Good question. Why not? And I thought, *I just can't. I can't remember the right words to say or the right way to stand. I can't smile or laugh with them. I can't pretend.*

I had run out of excuses. I said, "Because my dad had to go back to Mexico."

"When's he coming back?"

I shrugged. They thought he could just get on a plane and come back. They didn't know he would have to cross the desert again. They didn't know that I crossed it with him and Mamá and Dalia, before Reina was born. There was a secret part of me that they didn't know about, that I would never tell them.

Then one day at lunch, after I didn't laugh at Morgan's joke about the cafeteria lady's gigantic Easter bunny earrings, my friends dumped me.

"Zitlally turned boring," Olivia said to Emma and Morgan in a loud whisper.

Sometimes I used to wonder what would happen if I stopped trying. This was it. I picked up my orange tray and moved to another table, an empty one, and decided to let myself turn more and more boring until I became nothing at all.

I found Star in the forest exactly two weeks after Papá was deported. I know because that first night, the moon was disappearing just like I wanted to disappear. But the next night, a sliver appeared, and each night after that, the moon grew and grew until it was full and perfect. And when I saw that moon full and perfect and not missing even the tiniest sliver, I fell asleep hoping that something good might happen.

The next day after school, I ran to the forest. Along the trail, little yellow flowers were pushing through. Daffodils. Someone, sometime had planted ruffly, sunshiny daffodils in the car part forest, and this cheered me up a little. I went under the gate and over the ditch and the tears were already coming because they'd been waiting all day, just pushing against their hiding places, and they couldn't wait to come out.

And then I spotted him.

Gray fur.

It was supposed to be white but it was dirty and matted in places with brown stuff so he blended into the car part forest, like a chameleon. He was skinny, too. You could see the outline of his rib bones.

Usually, I am not a dog person. I have a scar the size of a blueberry on my thigh and another on my arm from where a dog bit me in Mexico when I was five.

But this dog seemed scared of me. Of *me*. He

whimpered and cowered and walked in a circle and curled up far from me, under a rusty rainbow truck hood. There was a chain tight around his neck and it was attached to a hole in the hood and he barely had enough chain to make the circle and lie down.

By now my tears had already come and I couldn't go back, so I sat far from him and he watched me and I watched him. I cried and he watched me and after a while my tears stopped and he put his head on his paws. That's when I noticed it. A black patch of fur on the back of his neck.

In the shape of a star.

· 2 ·

The next day after school, I went to the forest.
This time the tears weren't pushing, because I was
thinking about Star. Would he still be there? Was
he okay?

I whizzed by crushed beer cans and Burger King
trash and the daffodils. Their petals were a little
more open today.

There he was! Under the rusty rainbow truck hood.

I sat closer to him than I had the day before. There was a dirty puddle of rainwater that he kept trying to reach with his tongue, but his chain wouldn't let him. He made a high-pitched, desperate sound.

Nearby, a plastic bowl lay on its side, but it was cracked. I remembered the Burger King trash in the ditch. I said, "I'll be right back, Star."

I ran back and found the tall Burger King cup, and I tore off the top so that a dog's tongue could reach in, and carefully, inch by inch, I moved toward the puddle. But I didn't have to worry because he stayed back, far from me.

I scooped up water into the cup and put it on the other side of the puddle, so he could reach it. And then, quickly, I backed up, so quickly I stumbled in the mud. Then I sat against a torn-off truck door and watched.

Slowly, very slowly, he moved toward the cup,

reached out a perfect pink tongue, and lapped it up, politely, without spilling a drop.

After that came Saturday, and Dalia and Reina and I had to move our stuff into Mamá's room and clean our room for two guys to come live in it. We couldn't afford rent on the trailer now that Papá was *deportado*, so we had to rent out the room. The guys who moved in were drywallers. They each brought a garbage bag full of clothes in one hand and a six-pack of beer in the other. They dumped the bags in their new room, then sat on the sofa watching action movies and playing video games and drinking Coronas. Mamá's lips made a tight, upside-down parenthesis, and she cleaned up the kitchen as fast as she could and then went into our room and watched *telenovelas* and *noticias* on the bed while we did homework.

There's one more thing. On the day Papá found out he was going to be *deportado*, it was my eleventh birthday. There was a cake waiting for me in the fridge, a *tres leches* cake from Albertson's that said *Feliz Cumpleaños Zitlaly*. They missed the third *L*.

That night, all anyone talked about was *deportado deportado* and so my cake sat in the fridge, uneaten.

You have to be happy to sing *"Las Mañanitas"* and have a party, and nobody was happy. A few times over the next three weeks, Reina asked if she could eat some cake, but Mamá frowned at her. Mamá frowned a lot nowadays. She had to work extra hours, cooking the breakfast and lunch shift at IHOP and the dinner shift at Denny's. She wasn't home when we got home from school anymore. And she worked weekends now, too.

At three o'clock on that Saturday, Mamá walked past the drywall guys on the sofa and left for Denny's. In our crowded room, Reina was still watching TV and Dalia was sulking on the bed because she wanted to be with her friends at the broken-glass park. Luckily, Mamá thought I was too young to look after Reina myself, so Dalia had to do it.

After Mamá left, I snuck into the kitchen and heaved the box of cake out of the refrigerator. It was enormous. No one noticed me and the cake going out the door.

On the way to the forest, I had to grip my hands tight around it. It was especially hard going under the fence and jumping across the ditch with the cake. I didn't want it to get smushed or anything.

Star saw me coming with the cake and then he did something amazing.

He wagged his tail.

He wagged it!

My heart was booming. I sat down closer to him and balanced the white cake box on my lap, a little afraid to open the top. What if the cake was covered in green mold? What if it was ruined?

I lifted off the top.

Dazzling white with bright blue icing trim. A blue like pictures of the ocean in Hawaii. One side was a little mashed from when I'd tripped over a rock, and the icing was cracked and hard, but at least there was no mold. Could you get sick from eating really old cake? I decided to risk it. I didn't have a knife or fork so I just broke off a piece with my hand and took a bite. It tasted good. Dry, but good.

I made a silent prayer-bargain. *If I don't get a stomachache from this, then Papá will come back.* I took a few more bites. My stomach felt fine.

Star was watching me and licking his chops. It was probably safe to give him. Chocolate could hurt dogs but this was all pure white and blue. I tore off a big chunk that included the Z of *Zitlally*. He liked it so much I gave him two more pieces. We watched each other and ate the cake and the fur around his mouth turned blue and I smiled at him and stuck out my tongue to show him the blueness. I could see the tip of it if I kind of crossed my eyes and looked down. It looked like I'd licked off a piece of the ocean.

When I looked up again, I swear, Star smiled back.

· 3 ·

No one ever made fun of my name until that Monday. Cayden called me Zitface. "Zitlally, Zitface, Zitlally, Zitface."

I don't even have any zits. Not a single one.

I didn't say anything. I was used to not talking by now. When Mr. Martin asked me about it, I made some coughing sounds and whispered that I had a permanent sore throat from allergies. He raised his eyebrow and said maybe I should talk to Mrs. Cruz, the counselor, but then another teacher came in asking for the key to something and he forgot about it. Which was fine because Mrs. Cruz smells weird because she drinks about ten cups of coffee a day.

So when Cayden said "Zitface" again, I chewed on the insides of my cheeks and studied my knuckles and wondered how it would feel to punch a person.

Then Crystal said to him, "Dude, Zitlally's face is perfect. Like a movie star's. Like some model in a magazine."

My cheeks turned warm.

Then she said, "Dude, I know Zitlally's family. They live next door to me. She comes from a family of models. Like, all her aunts and cousins are models. But there are, like, these gangs there in Mexico, enemy gangs of beautiful models, so Zitlally's family had to flee. It was tragic. It was like they were just too beautiful."

Cayden screwed up his face. "You're such a liar, Crystal."

She *was* a liar. Everyone knew not to believe nine-tenths of what came out of Crystal's mouth. Most of her lies were just good stories, but it was hard to get past the fact that she was lying. Still, Cayden didn't call me Zitface again.

Two class periods later, during a science experiment about static electricity, Crystal was rubbing a balloon on her hair. Dirty-blond strands stuck out in all directions. She looked like a lying lunatic. But her wild hair also looked a little like a golden halo that you might see around the Virgin Mary's head, the thing that shows she's holy.

Crystal stuck the balloon to the wall, and there it stayed, a little miracle, like walking on water or multiplying loaves of bread or something.

From across the room, she looked at me and smiled. I smiled back and even let some teeth show.

Did she really think I looked like a model? It was possible. Every once in a while, you do see a brown-skinned model. I walked a little taller that day, threw back my shoulders, and pursed out my lips in a bee-stung model's pout.

The cake lasted three days. I didn't want to give it to Star all at once in case it made him sick. His stomach had probably shrunk, since he was starving. By the fourth day, maybe it was my imagination, but I swear he looked healthier, more meat on his bones, less space between his ribs. And he had a ring of blue fur around his mouth like lipstick.

There's something I didn't tell you about Papá being *deportado*. I didn't tell you because I wanted you to think he's a good person. Because he is. But if I told you right away that the reason the police pulled him over was because he was speeding, then you might think he's bad.

Even Mamá thinks he's bad. Not all the time, but sometimes. He always promised Mamá he wouldn't drive fast because if he got caught, he'd be *deportado*. But he went fishing in the mountains and caught the biggest trout in the Poudre River. Maybe even in *any* river. And on the way home, he was so happy he was singing along with the *ranchera* music on the radio. He was so happy he didn't notice the needle going up past thirty-five all the way to fifty. Next thing he knew there were flashing red and blue lights in his rearview. And all his happiness disappeared like that.

So that's why Mamá is so mad she won't take his phone calls from the little phone booth store in Xono, Mexico. That's why she won't send him two thousand dollars to pay for the coyote to bring him back across.

Emma and Morgan and Olivia wouldn't understand. They would think, *Oh my god, your dad is an illegal criminal speeder construction worker immigrant!*

But that's not who he is.

He is a man who whispers to me in star

language, in the language of an ancient civilization that built pyramids for the sun and the moon and tracked the patterns of stars.

Papá's favorite thing in the world is mushroom picking. I don't remember too much from Xono, but I remember when he took me mushroom hunting. It smelled like rain and mud, and the ground squished beneath our feet, and it was just me and him because Dalia didn't like walking very far.

The last time we went mushroom hunting together, I was six. We were deep in the forest, where hardly any people ever go, and he said, "Zitlally, why don't you look behind that rock there?" I did, and there was a sunset-colored mushroom that I dropped in my bag. I collected little sticks and he found big logs and we built a fire. We drank from a thermos of tea and roasted mushrooms on sticks over the fire. And then, after they cooled, I felt like I was eating little magical pieces of forest.

Once our bellies were full and happy, he said, "Zitlally, your *mamá* and I are going to *el Norte*."

I leaped into his lap, held his arm fiercely. "I'm coming, too," I said. Lots of kids in Xono lived with their grandparents or aunts or uncles because their parents were working in *el Norte*. My worst nightmare was that Dalia and I would become two of those kids.

He looked at me for a while and said, "Can you walk for a long, long time, Zitlally?"

"Yes!"

"Can you walk through a desert that is hotter than you can imagine in the day?"

"Yes!"

"And colder than you can imagine at night?"

"Yes!"

"And not complain?"

"Yes!"

"Can you walk at night and not be scared?"

I paused and then said, "I can try."

"Can you be quieter than a mouse and if I say *suelo* can you drop to the ground and shut your eyes tight so *la migra* can't see the light shining off them?"

"Yes, Papá. I'll do anything! *Please* take me with you!"

And he did.

Now my memories of Xono are broken pieces, like a plate that you dropped and you only saved a few shards and lost the rest. The best pieces, the ones I look at again and again, are the days we went mushroom hunting.

Now that Papá was back in Xono, he would get to go mushroom hunting. But that wouldn't happen till summer. He said mushroom hunting was only good during the rainy season. I wondered what he was doing instead. There were hardly any jobs there except teaching elementary school, which he couldn't do because he never finished elementary school. As a kid, he had to work in cornfields all day. Maybe he was working in the cornfields now. That was one of the only other jobs in Xono.

Mamá said he was probably sitting in the shade of a tree, fishing, and no way was she going to send her hard-earned money to him. I hoped summer would hurry up and come so he could pick the sunset-colored mushrooms and sell them at the market and make enough money to come home.

Every day the next week, I ran to the car part forest to see Star. Along the path, the daffodils were all the way opened up, starbursts of bright yellow petals around light yellow ones. Stars everywhere. A good sign. *Maybe Papá is coming home soon.*

Now Star wagged not just his tail but his whole butt when he saw me. Sometimes I brought him some slices of ham and bread, or tortillas spread with refried beans, or whatever I found in the fridge.

One day I brought him a chicken drumstick. That was the day I first touched him.

He finished the drumstick, even the bones, and then drank fresh water from a bowl I'd brought him. He looked so happy and kept pulling on his chain to come near me, sticking out his pink tongue like he wanted to lick me more than anything.

I took a deep breath and stretched out my hand. He licked and licked and licked. At first he probably wanted to lick off every last trace of chicken grease. But then he just kept on licking, like all the love he had for me was stored up in those licks. I let him lick my hand and then moved closer and he licked up to my elbow.

I laughed. I laughed and it was a strange sound in the forest of car scraps.

The next day, I stuck out my hand and let it rest on the fur on his back. I moved my hand around in his fur. He took a deep breath and put his head on his paws and sighed like he was in heaven.

The day after that, I hugged him. First I leaned against him. Then I put my face in his fur. It didn't matter that he was dirty. He had the most perfect dog smell. And for some reason, the tears came, even though they'd been hiding for a while. They came and he licked them from my face and I laughed.

I wanted to untie him, let him run free. I started to unhook the chain, then I stopped. What if he ran away and didn't come back? What if I got in trouble? What if his owner called the cops and they came to our trailer and asked for our papers?

I took my hand off Star's chain and scratched his ears. He smiled and leaned into my hand. What was Star doing in the forest anyway? Was someone in Forest View Mobile Home Park his owner? Then why wouldn't they keep Star on their property? Maybe they weren't allowed to have dogs? But if they wanted one so badly, wouldn't they take better care of him? Or maybe this was their property? Maybe I was a trespasser?

On Sunday afternoon, I was hugging Star when I heard a noise. Footsteps. Someone was coming down the path.

I froze.

Star's owner! I thought. Then I thought, *Or one of the gang guys!* But they usually stayed in the broken-glass playground. Unless, this time, they saw me come here and followed me.

I wondered if Star could protect me. He was probably strong now from all the cake and ham and chicken I gave him. He would defend me.

PART TWO

Crystal

· 4 ·

Through the metal scraps, a figure appeared. A girl. A scrappy, skinny girl with dirty-blond hair flying around her face.

Crystal.

"Hey, Zitlally," she said.

I stared. It felt like she'd snuck up on me in my own room, like she was trespassing on my territory.

"I know you never talk anymore," she said. "But that's okay because I can talk enough for both of us. Whose dog is that?"

I shrugged.

"It needs a bath pretty bad."

"He."

"What?"

"He's a he. See?"

"Oh, right." And she went up to him and scratched him behind the ears. Just like that.

Star half closed his eyes like he was in ecstasy. I was a little jealous.

"Hey, doggers," she said. "What's your name? Diggety? Doggety?"

"He's Star," I said. I kind of wished she would leave because what if Star liked her better? And worse, what if the tears started coming again? I kept my arms around Star.

Crystal kept scratching his neck. "Star's cool. But isn't it kind of a girl's name? Isn't that what your name means?"

"How do you know that?"

"Remember? Fourth-grade name project last year? We made those posters?"

"Oh, right."

She put her finger against her lips, thinking. "I bet in humans, Star's a girl's name, but in dogs, it's a boy's name."

I shrugged.

She kept petting Star and talking. "I saw you come down here and I wondered what you were up to. My mom's boyfriend's out of work now and he's always in a crabby mood. He used to be a dictator of some island way out in the middle of nowhere. Out past Hawaii. He was so evil they overthrew him and excommunicated him. And he has so many enemies that are always trying to assassinate him that he had to go into hiding in this Forest View craphole."

She talked and talked and sometimes a bee buzzed between us and a bird flew around here and there. The air was honey sweet and filled with spring and I didn't even need a sweater. I was warm enough hugging Star. Little by little, I

35

stopped worrying Star would like her better. After all, who saved him from starvation?

Anyway, a star belongs with a star.

Crystal and I walked back together. Emma was wrong. Crystal didn't have chronic halitosis. Her breath smelled like Coke and Fritos, in a good way. She might shop at garage sales, though, judging by her outfit—jeans that were too short and too blue and had a flower patch on the knee (not the cool kind that came with the pants, but the kind that someone sewed over a hole). Her sweater had sparkly silver threads woven through, which made it look like sunshine on tiny waves of a river. Up close, though, you could see how it was old and nubby, and worn at the elbows, and stained with something yellow near the neckline.

In front of our trailers, you could hear the dictator boyfriend yelling. The TV was blaring Animal Planet, a show about penguins—you could hear it all the way outside between his cussing. I said goodbye to Crystal and went inside my trailer. Even from inside, with the door closed, you could still hear the dictator yelling. It made me dig my fingernails into my palms.

The drywaller guys had come home early from work since it was Sunday. They were camped out on the sofa, all covered in white dust, as though someone had dumped powdered sugar over them. They didn't smell like donuts, though. They smelled like sweaty socks and beer. They ignored me as I got a snack in the kitchen and went into the bedroom to turn on Animal Planet. Penguins were waddling and the announcer was saying that Antarctica was the harshest place to live on earth.

And I thought, *I'm not so sure about that.* Compared to Crystal's trailer, Antarctica looked pretty peaceful, all still and dazzling white, like fresh icing on a *tres leches* cake.

I had to start doing a good job on my homework because Mr. Martin had called Mamá. I don't know exactly what he told her, but his Spanish was good, so I knew she understood. Afterward she said in a cold Antarctic voice, "Zitlally, if your grades don't improve and if you don't start talking more at school I'm sending you back to Mexico with your father."

Part of me thought of Star in the forest and how sad he would be if I left. And how I would miss Dalia and Reina even though I didn't like them too much.

But part of me thought, *Good! Then Papá and I can go mushroom hunting together and he can star whisper.*

Then Mamá said, "And you'd have to stop going to school in three years because there's no high school in our *pueblo*. You'd have to be a maid and wash clothes by hand for two dollars a day."

I decided to do better in school.

On Monday, I forced myself to talk more. I raised my hand and answered questions and when Mr. Martin was around I looked for Crystal and let her start talking to me so it looked like I had friends so he wouldn't call Mamá back.

Crystal was there, scratching Star's ears, when I got to the forest. She started talking and talking about how her dad was on an Antarctic expedition studying penguins and there was a giant ice storm and their lines of communication broke and she suspected he was floating on a piece of a glacier in the middle of the sea. I knew she ripped it off Animal Planet, but it was a good story, so I listened and said, "Wow."

When Star saw me, he wiggled out of her grasp and pulled on his chain toward me. I ran to him and he licked me all up and down my arms. I gave him a big chunk of cheese and hugged him. Now I didn't feel jealous at all, just warm inside because it was obvious he liked me better.

He liked me so much he probably would have kept licking me if I'd unhooked his chain. But even thinking about him running away and forgetting about me and never coming back made me want to cry. No. He had to stay on the chain. For his own good.

"I'm glad we're best friends," Crystal said.

"Best friends?"

"I mean, coming here with you and talking

with you at school and everything. The other girls are really stuck-up, you know? Like those girls you used to hang with—Morgan and Emma and all. They're boring, you know?" She pretended to yawn.

Then she said, "I used to think they just liked you 'cause you're pretty."

I wasn't sure what to say to that.

But she kept talking. "Now I know it's 'cause you're nice. And you listen good." She smiled, and said again, "Yep, I sure am glad we're best friends." Like if she said it enough it might become true.

It was a little nice that she was happy being my best friend, even though she wasn't, really. She pretended she was, though. It was another one of her lies. I decided to just go along with it.

One day, after a week of coming to the forest with me, Crystal rubbed Star's belly and sighed, "Your dog is so great. I wish I had a dog like him."

Your dog. That's what she said. *Your dog.* And

it's true, Star was my dog, even though I had no idea how he got there, under the rusty truck hood. There was someone else out there, someone like an evil dictator, who thought Star was *his* dog. Who had a different name for Star, a wrong name.

"Let's take Star off the chain," Crystal said.

My insides twisted up. "What if he runs away?"

"He won't."

"What if we get in trouble?"

"Who cares?"

I didn't feel brave enough. "I don't feel like it now," I said. "Another day, maybe."

Crystal didn't argue with me because Star was mine.

At dinnertime, Crystal said, "See ya, Zit!" and I didn't mind. I just pouted out my lips like a beautiful model hiding a tragic secret and said, "Bye."

On Saturday, I got to the forest and Crystal wasn't there.

I hugged Star and fed him and he gave me kisses all over my face. I whispered to him in star

41

language and he liked it but he kept looking around, looking for Crystal.

I felt myself looking around, too. The air felt empty, like some of the springtime had been sucked out of it. I think Star noticed it, too.

Crystal was not at the bus stop or in school on Monday. I wondered if she was sick. Their beat-up, junk-filled car wasn't parked in front of their trailer.

That afternoon, Star and I hung out alone again.

That night, no lights or Animal Planet sounds came from Crystal's windows. There was a terrible storm, the kind with thunder that makes you jump right out of bed. I stayed awake, long after Mamá and Dalia and Reina were asleep, all their raspy breaths overlapping each other.

I thought about Star in the storm and I hoped he was curled up under the rusty hood and wasn't too scared and lonely.

I wondered where Crystal had gone and if

she'd come back and if there was a storm where she was.

I wondered if there was a storm in Xono, too. Rainy season would start in June, around when school ended. I remembered the storms in rainy season. I remembered being in the kitchen, which was a bamboo shack with slits of light coming through, and woodsmoke filling the space, and the room flashing with lightning, and Papá setting me on his lap and wrapping himself around me so I wouldn't feel scared.

Papá was good at making me not scared.

After the dog bit me in Xono when I was five, two things happened. I got scared of the dark. And I started waking up in the middle of the night, having to pee really bad.

That was a big problem because to get to our outhouse, you had to walk through a creepy patch of woods. Dalia went with me at first and complained the whole time. "Zitlally! It takes a hundred years for your pee to come out."

43

That was another problem. I was so scared in that outhouse, I couldn't pee. I sat there and held the flashlight and shivered at the giant bug shadows. No pee came out. Dalia yelled at me from outside. "Come on, Zitlally! I'm freezing!" She threw back the curtain and glared. "I thought you had to pee!"

After Dalia wouldn't take me anymore, Papá did. With his eyes half open, he picked up the flashlight and held my hand and creaked, "Let's go, *m'hija*."

At the edge of the patch of woods, I stopped and listened to the howls and moans of hidden creatures. I squeezed his hand. "What if there's a mean dog in there?"

Instead of rolling his eyes and pushing me and snapping "*Go!*" like Dalia did, he bent down and picked up a stick. It was as long as my arm, with some pointy nubs. "If a mean dog comes, *m'hija*, then hold up this magic stick. He'll run away with his tail between his legs."

I gripped the stick tight. Just holding it made the howls and moans disappear. And with the howls and moans gone, I could hear the cricket chirps, and a softer sound between them. Stars whispering. Now that I didn't have to look for mean dog shadows in the woods, I could watch the moon shadows stretching in front of me and Papá. Big, tall, strong shadows.

Inside the outhouse, I sat on the wooden seat, holding my magic stick. Outside the curtain, Papá was whistling a low, starry tune just loud enough that I knew he was there. The pee flowed right out.

For a while, every night after that, Papá handed me a stick, a new one each time. He could always find magic sticks, even in the dark. Now that I'm eleven, I don't believe in magic sticks, but I have to admit, they worked.

In jail, when I saw Papá looking small and scared through the plastic window, I wanted a magic stick. Even with those square ceiling lights above, it felt dark in there, like it was the middle of the night and we were in the woods packed with mean dogs. I wanted Papá to find me a magic stick. And I wondered, if he couldn't find one, could I find one myself? Could I find one for both of us?

· 5 ·

Three days passed before Crystal came back. I peeked at the note from her mom on Mr. Martin's desk. *Family emergency,* it said.

At recess, Crystal stood alone by the fence.

I walked over and said, "Where were you?"

She sighed, a big long sigh. "The dictator left. His enemies found out where he was hiding, so he took off. Probably to conquer another island. So me and my mom went to look for my dad."

"In Antarctica?" I asked. Really, sometimes her lies went too far. I mean, you couldn't even *get* to Antarctica in four days.

"Of course not. He just got back and we had to meet him at the airport. They located his research team with one of those GPS things. So we stayed with him at this fancy hotel for a few days, but now they're sending him out on another mission. Africa this time. Madagascar. Studying lemurs."

"Lemurs?"

"You know, like monkeys."

"Oh, right. Lemurs."

Later that day, in the forest, Crystal asked, "What about *your* father?"

"What about him?"

"I haven't seen him around."

I tried to think of something as glamorous as Antarctica or Madagascar, but my brain couldn't invent lies as fast as hers. "He had to go back to Mexico."

"What's he doing there?"

"In the summer he'll pick mushrooms. They have good ones in the forest there. It's like looking for treasures. They're really rare and valuable." And it was true, they were. If you sold them at the market you could get a lot of money. But we never sold them. We roasted them and ate them and felt like royalty.

"Cool."

"And I used to go with him, and I had a really good eye for spotting them." Although thinking about it now, I realized he probably spotted the mushrooms and told me where to look.

"What'd they look like?" she asked.

"Some are red and orange like a sunset. Some are blue green like the ocean. There's all different kinds."

Crystal looked at me long and hard. "You should talk more. You have good stuff to say."

* * *

The next day at school, Crystal said under her breath in the lunch line, as though it was top-secret, "Don't come to Star right after school. Wait until four o'clock, okay?"

"Why?"

"Just trust me, okay?"

"Okay."

I watched TV until 3:50. Well, really I watched the clock on the DVD player that seemed to go so, so slowly I thought it was broken. I was by myself. I was hardly ever alone in the house and the air felt strange with no one else in it. Even the TV noise couldn't fill the space.

Yesterday, Dalia and Mamá had gotten in a big fight and Dalia said she was moving in with her boyfriend and dropping out of school and Mamá said, "No you aren't, you're only sixteen," and Dalia said, "I'll do whatever I want to do."

Then late that night, Dalia moved all her clothes and makeup and stuff into a trailer on the other side of Forest View, and she wasn't talking to Mamá and wouldn't answer the cell phone when she called. So Reina stayed after school the next day with a neighbor lady. Luckily I am the perfect age. Mamá says I'm a year too young to babysit my sister, because who knows what the laws are in this country and the last thing she needs is the police coming and arresting her for leaving a four-year-old with an eleven-year-old.

But eleven is old enough to wander around the neighborhood without the neighbor lady knowing what you're up to. I told her I was going to play with Crystal and she didn't ask any more questions, just went back to her *telenovelas* while Reina messed with the remote control with no batteries.

Finally 3:50 came and I ran to the forest. Crystal was sitting next to Star. She looked excited about something, so excited she was about to burst. She jumped up when she saw me. She rocked back and forth on her heels with a giant smile. "Zitlally! Guess what?"

"What?"

"You're going mushroom hunting today!"

And she handed me a basket, the kind with a handle that fancy bottles of bubble bath come in. Papá and I always just used plastic bags, so the basket made me feel like Little Red Riding Hood, but Crystal was so wound up it didn't matter.

"Okay, go!" she squealed. "Look for them."

"But they don't grow here," I said. "And even if I found a mushroom, I wouldn't know if it was poisonous or anything."

"Just look!" she shouted.

First I fed Star his cheese and petted him.

"Come on!" she said. "Go!"

I picked up the basket, unsure what to do.

"Look behind that tire, Zitlally, look!"

I peeked behind the tire and spotted a plastic Ziploc bag, and inside, a red and orange mushroom. It was the small kind that they sell here in the stores, the gray kind, but this was orangey red. I took it from the bag and held it close to my face.

Crystal ran up behind me. "Look! It's sunset colored! Eat it! You can eat it!"

I looked at her doubtfully.

"It's just food coloring. The red and the orange! I did it myself!"

I took a little bite. It tasted like Styrofoam, like all store mushrooms do. Not like the broken-plate memory I had of mushrooms roasted over a fire back in Mexico. I forced myself to eat the whole thing.

"There's more!" she screamed. "Look some more."

I looked around, under the bits of worn scrap metal, inside old hubcaps, and sure enough, there they were, hidden in nooks and crannies. Mushrooms in plastic bags, dyed ocean blue and green and sunset orange.

"I put them in plastic bags to be sanitary!"

I offered her one and she took it, grimacing as she ate it. "Needs salt," she said.

I found all nine mushrooms and put them in

my basket, except one, which I gave to Star. He nibbled at it to be polite.

"I'll eat the rest at home," I said. "With salt."

"And maybe mustard," she said.

We started walking home down the path.

"And chocolate," I said.

"Oooh! I know! You should microwave a Snickers on them."

The whole way back we planned dyed-mushroom recipes.

"Thanks, Crystal," I said before she went into her trailer.

She smiled. "That's what best friends are for." And she went inside.

First I thought, *You're not my best friend.* Then I thought about how she took all that time to dye the mushrooms and hide them and how she did it for me, just to make me happy.

As I turned to go to my trailer, I heard her mom yelling. I could make out the words perfectly. "You left a frickin' mess in here! Food dye everywhere!" Something bashed. "I should've left you there with your dad, left you both to rot in jail."

Jail. Crystal's dad was in jail.

Just like my dad, only hers was still there. Her mom must have taken her to visit him because the boyfriend left. And here I was all wrapped up in feeling sorry for myself about Papá. Maybe things weren't so bad for me after all. Papá was probably whistling under a blue sky in a green cornfield, working hard to pay his way back to us. And he *would* come back. And Mamá would *never* go out and get herself an evil dictator boyfriend. Papá *was* coming back, and we would all be happy again.

Crystal was the one who really needed a magic stick. Something to make her feel safe. Strong. Loved.

Maybe her lies were her magic stick.

Maybe Star was.

Maybe I was.

· 6 ·

"We got to do it," Crystal said. "We got to unhook Star's chain."

It was Saturday and we'd brought a bucket of water, a cup, a raggedy towel, a bottle of orange shampoo-and-conditioner-in-one, scissors, and an old hairbrush that Dalia had left behind.

Crystal was right. We couldn't do a good job

washing Star if he was tied up. "He won't run away?" I said.

"No way. We're, like, his masters now. He's our best friend forever till death do us part. Like you and me."

I was glad I'd brought bacon. That was Star's favorite. I fried it especially for him. Even if he tried to run away, I was sure I could lure him back with bacon.

I held my breath and pushed on the chain's hook with my finger. The hook was rusty and kind of stuck, but I pushed as hard as I could until it moved. Then I pulled the chain from it and held my breath.

Star was free. He sat there, wagging his tail, smiling at me.

"See, Zit?" Crystal said. "Told you."

I scratched his ears and said, "Good Star. Good, good Star," while Crystal poured water over his fur. He squirmed a little, but he stayed. He looked smaller all wet, and you could still see some long bumps that were his ribs. We lathered him up until he smelled like a big, fresh piece of orange Starburst. Then we rinsed him and dried him with the towel. With scissors, Crystal cut out the tangled, matted pieces of fur. Luckily he had enough fur that the rest filled in the gaps.

"I'm just going to layer his hair a little," Crystal said. She walked around him, fluffing his fur here and there, studying it like a hairdresser about to try a new style.

"He already looks good like this," I said.

"Listen, Zit. A few years back, my mom was, like, the owner of this chain of super-fancy beauty salons. She taught me everything she knows. I'm a whiz at layers. I can give his hair a windblown look."

I snatched the scissors from Crystal's hands and stuck the brush there. "You can brush and style. But absolutely no layers!"

"No problem," she said. "I can work magic with a brush."

At first I didn't believe her because of her

scraggly mess of hair. But as she styled Star's fur, I had to admit, it looked like she knew what she was doing. And Star was sighing with delight the whole time. Maybe Crystal's mom had worked at the Supercuts in the mall for a while or something.

When Crystal was done, she said, "Tah-dah!"

Star seemed to hold his head higher, like he was proud of his new look. He did look sensational. His fur was white as the moon. The star on his head was black as the night. We ran around and played with him. I admit I was nervous he'd take off, but he never left our sight. When it was time to go, we hugged him goodbye and hooked him back up to the chain. "*Hasta mañana*, Star," I said, and blew him a kiss.

On the way back from the forest, Crystal said, "Tell me a story, Zit."

That was a first. It was as though she was out of her own stories. Luckily, I did have plenty of stories: stories Papá would tell me.

"About what?" I asked.

"About, um . . ." She looked at Star. "Animals."

I thought. "Well," I said, "my dad told me how in the time of the great-great-grandparents, people used to have special animals. When a baby was born, they'd figure out what its special animal was. And if something happened to the animal, like it got shot, then the person would get hurt, too. He would feel the animal's pain. And if the animal died, the person died, too."

"That's awful!" Crystal said.

"But also," I said, "if a person needed extra strength, like superpowers, he could think about his animal and use its powers. Like if it was a deer, he could run really fast."

Crystal was nodding and thinking and listening closely. "So their fates were tied up together."

I nodded.

"You think Star is someone's animal?" she whispered. "That there's some human out there who has his same fate?"

I shrugged.

But inside, I knew. I knew who shared Star's fate. I'd known ever since the day he wagged his tail at me. And every time he licked me, I felt more sure. It wasn't just a coincidence that I met Star right after Papá left. Papá must have asked his special animal to stay with me.

This made me feel good.

But Star was illegal, too, like Papá. No license, no papers. If the dog cops came, I couldn't prove Star was really mine. And if the person who thought he was Star's owner took him, there was nothing I could do. This scared me. Star could disappear at any time, just like Papá.

When I got home, the drywallers were still at work, and my sisters were watching TV in the living room. Mamá and Dalia had started talking again because Dalia had broken up with her boyfriend and said she wanted to come home. We'd all missed her a lot anyway, and she did help out with Reina after school.

Mamá was zipping around the kitchen, frying meat and heating beans and tortillas for dinner. She wore a short jeans skirt and a silky black top and dangly golden earrings. And she was wrapped up in a haze of perfume that nearly drowned out the sizzling meat smell.

"Where are you going?" I asked. She was too dressed up for work.

"Out with my girlfriends. Dalia's watching you and Reina." She was stirring and flipping and grabbing cups and forks so fast she didn't even look at me. "I'll be back late."

This made me red-hot furious. *What?!* I wanted to scream. *Reina and I aren't good enough to hang out with on a Saturday night?!*

I decided I wouldn't talk to her.

She snatched a plate with one hand. With the other hand, she scooped out beans and slid some meat onto the plate. She did the same with three more plates, then plopped them on the table. "Dalia! Reina! Dinner!"

I picked at my beans and didn't say a single

word to Mamá. Not even *Pass the salt.* I didn't even nod or shake my head. Reina went on and on about Dora the Explorer and her magical stars while I glared at Mamá from the corner of my eye.

She didn't notice. She scarfed down her food, wiped her mouth, grabbed her purse, and called out good night over her shoulder. The screen door slammed behind her, and I started thinking, *Maybe I should start getting bad grades so Mr. Martin will call her and she'll send me back to Mexico to live with Papá.* But when I thought of that, my stomach tightened into a hundred thousand knots.

Papá's truck is red with an American flag on one window and a Mexican flag on the other. It says *Mora* in big, fancy letters across the back windshield because that's our last name. He used to wash his truck every Sunday after church and Reina and I would help.

The week after Dalia moved back in, Reina got sick with a fever and white spots all over her throat. So we all got in the truck, Reina and Dalia and Mamá and me, and we went to Urgent Care. It turned out Reina had strep throat, and we had to drive to the pharmacy to pick up her medicine. On the way to the pharmacy, Reina was asleep and Dalia was listening to music on her earphones and Mamá was telling me how we'd have to mix the medicine with Coke so Reina would take it.

That's when I noticed it.

The red flashing light, and then the siren, right behind us.

My heart started booming.

Then Mamá noticed the light and the siren. She stopped talking about the medicine and started saying, "*Jesús María José Jesús María José . . .*" She pulled over and whispered the names of the entire Holy Family over and over and over again until the cop came to her window.

"License, insurance, and registration, ma'am."

She opened the glove compartment. Her hands were shaking bad. She held out the pieces of paper. They were shaking bad, too.

The cop watched the papers shaking, like it was proof she was guilty.

She said in English, "I forget license. In my home. I very sorry, very sorry, mister."

My face got hot. She talked like a baby in English. Plus, she was lying about the license. She never lied, but now she was lying.

The cop talked slowly, like she was a little kid. "Ma'am, it's against the law to drive without a license. If you can't locate it, I recommend you get a new one or stay off the roads." He stared at her hard, like he knew she was illegal. Like she was a stray dog without tags, something you would send to the pound, except it wouldn't be the pound, it would be Mexico.

Tears started pouring out of her eyes, and my hot feeling got hotter. I looked at Dalia. Her face was stony. Her earphones were in her lap and her fingers were twisting around the wires.

This is it.

We're all going to be deportadas *now and they'll*

send us straight to jail, then straight to Mexico, and will I have time to say goodbye to Star and even Crystal, because yes, maybe she's my best friend after all, and maybe she'll take care of Star, I know she will, and what about Reina, because she was born here and she's legal and what if they make her stay and make us go, because even though she's a pain sometimes, I like having her around, and who will make sure she takes all ten days of antibiotics and know that you have to mix it with a little Coke for her to swallow it?

The cop said, "Ma'am, are you aware you have a headlight out?"

Mamá didn't understand. My mouth was stuck shut, so Dalia translated.

"No, mister," Mamá said. "I don't know light broken."

He gave her back the little pieces of paper. "It's your lucky day, ma'am. Just promise me you'll get that headlight fixed. And stay off the roads if you don't have a license."

"Yes, yes, mister, thank you, thank you." Except she said it like *Tank you*. But I didn't feel too embarrassed this time because I was so glad we weren't going to be *deportadas*.

By the time we got home, my heart had stopped booming enough that I could do my social studies homework and only once in a while did a picture come into my head of Mamá's hands shaking.

The next day, Mamá said her heart kept booming, like it was stuck, like when a clock alarm's beeping and you can't find the Off button. Finally, she said she wasn't going to drive anymore in this country because it was giving her *nervios*. And she started saying she missed Papá, and maybe she'd send him that money if he swore not to speed again.

For a few days, Papá's red truck sat in front of our trailer, looking lonely. I passed it every day on the way to the bus stop, and coming home from the bus stop, and on the way to the forest, and on the way home from the forest. I brushed my hand against it every time I passed, and a thin layer of dirt rubbed off on my fingertips.

After church on Sunday, we were walking home from the bus stop when I saw the drywaller guys peeling off the Mora sticker with a knife. They were putting on a sticker of a beautiful lady in a swimsuit instead.

Mamá frowned at the new sticker, but she didn't tell them to get their hands off Papá's truck.

I pressed my lips together, tight and furious.

Inside, Mamá started scrambling eggs.

I couldn't hold it in anymore. "Did you sell Papá's truck to the drywall guys?"

"Yes."

"You want us to forget about him, don't you?"

"He's coming home, Zitlally," she said. And she smiled in a shiny-eyed way that made me sure she wasn't joking. "I sent the money from the truck to your father. Money to pay the coyote. He's coming home. Probably in a week or so. *Si Dios quiere.*"

I was so dizzy with happiness, I couldn't find words.

"We wanted it to be a surprise, Zitlally," she said. "We wanted him to just show up at the door and see how happy you'd be."

There was so much happiness in me now, the trailer was too small to hold it all. So much happiness it was bursting out the windows and through the screen door. So much happiness the only thing I could think to do with it all was grab some stale tortillas and run next door to Crystal's.

· 7 ·

Usually Crystal was the one who knocked on my door, but this time I knocked on hers. She answered the door in pink leggings and a purple T-shirt that was too big for her.

"My dad's coming home!" I said. "Want to go to the forest to celebrate?"

"Woohoo!" she shouted. "Woohoooooo!"

She put on some sparkly flip-flops and we took

off running down the path and I didn't even feel embarrassed that her outfit looked like pajamas. It was full-fledged springtime now. Red tulips with velvety black stars inside had opened up next to the daffodils.

When we got there, Star was wagging his tail like crazy. I gave him a hug and a tortilla and unhooked his chain.

"Hey!" Crystal said. "I got an idea!"

"What?"

"Let's train Star. We can put on a dog show for your dad!"

"You know how to train dogs?"

"Duh!" She said it in a nice way, though. "My dad trained like nineteen hundred sled dogs in Alaska a few years back. You know the ones in those races?"

I nodded.

"Well, he trained, like, all the winners. And he taught me, too." She nuzzled her nose against Star's. "Plus, we had a puppy once named Poopsies, and she peed everywhere and chewed up

71

everything and my mom's boyfriend said if Poopsies didn't get good fast he was gonna put her in a sack filled with stones and throw it in a river."

"That's awful!" Now that I thought about it, I remembered, a couple of years back, a puppy yapping and whining in their trailer.

"I know. If my dad was there he would have kicked the dictator's butt and made Poopsies into a blue-ribbon sled dog. But he was working with kangaroos in Australia, so I got out a bunch of books from the library and started training Poopsies myself."

"Did it work?"

"I practically got that dog to talk!" she said.

"Where's Poopsies now?" I asked.

Crystal looked away, at grass poking through an old engine. "With my dad. He fell in love with her since she was so well-behaved. So I said he could take her along on his trips. He gets sad sometimes without me, you know?"

I knew where her dad really was. But it seemed too late to tell her now. It seemed like something a person shouldn't do to her best friend. So I decided to let myself believe her dad really was a sled-dog-training, lemur-studying, polar-bear-saving world traveler. Who got sad sometimes.

Crystal must have learned something from those library books, because the first day of training, with just some Cheerios, we taught Star how to sit! And on the second day, with lemon wafers, how to lie down. And on the third day, with Doritos, how to roll over. He was such a smart dog.

The fourth day he learned how to shake hands. That was the day Papá called us to say he was in Sonora, right on the Mexican side of the border. He said he was going to cross over to Arizona that night, over to the American side. And then it would be just another day or two until he got home to Forest View.

Mamá made flan and hot chocolate that night to celebrate, and we all watched TV together in our room, feeling warm and cozy. Dalia didn't complain that it was a cartoon, and when Reina

73

got scared at the shark, we held her tight, and then we stayed like that, holding each other.

The next day, in the car part forest, when I told Crystal my dad was just on the other side of the border now, she screamed, "Woohooooo!"

"We have to teach Star something amazing, something to really impress your dad."

We looked around the car part forest for inspiration. Flowers, vines, weeds, trees, and lots of car parts. A squirrel ran along the hood of the truck cab and inside the open window. It sat on the steering wheel and made those funny chirping sounds, like it was trying to tell us something, an idea.

"I know!" I said. "My dad will probably be sad we sold his truck. So we can get Star to do a trick with this truck. Like stand on it or something."

"Or drive it!" Crystal said. She put her hand to the door's rusted handle. She had to pull with all her might to get it to creak open.

Star was a perfect student. A plus plus. He learned how to climb into the truck cab, and not only that. He put his paw on the horn and beeped it!

Crystal and I burst out laughing. We laughed so hard we fell to the ground and rolled around and didn't care how dirty our clothes were getting. We laughed and laughed, and when Star saw us laughing so hard, he beeped again and again.

"It really looks like he's driving!" I said between little gasps.

"Your dad's gonna be laughing so hard he'll pee in his pants!" Crystal said.

And then we laughed some more at that.

The next day was Friday, which meant that Papá was probably on our side of the border now and on his way to Colorado. All day in school, that's all I could think about. When Mr. Martin told me to read the next paragraph about amphibians, I didn't even know what page we were on. There was an awkward silence, but then Crystal called out, "Second paragraph on page thirty, Zitlally."

My face felt a little hot, but mostly I felt thankful, and I didn't care that everyone in the fifth grade thought she was my best friend now.

After school, we got together our bag of supplies to wash Star and make him look good for Papá. He'd already gotten a little dirty over the past week, but nowhere near as bad as before. "We'll just do a little touch-up," Crystal said. We filled the turquoise car-washing bucket halfway with water and brought it down the path toward the forest. We had to take turns carrying it because it was really heavy and the metal handle kept digging into our palms.

"Too bad there's not electricity there," Crystal said. "Then we could bring my mom's curling iron and totally style his hair."

"Yeah, too bad," I said, secretly glad there was no electricity. It would have been embarrassing for Star to have his hair curled. After all, he was a boy. I just wanted his fur to be clean and white so that the star on the back of his neck would stand out for Papá. And I wanted him to smell like an orange Starburst.

The tulips' petals were shriveling and turning brown at the edges now, and the daffodils' had already fallen off. Too bad Papá wouldn't get to see how pretty they looked when they were new and bright.

That's what I was thinking when we turned the corner into the car part forest and saw that Star was gone.

PART THREE

Papá

· 8 ·

For a long time, we looked for Star. We looked under every crumbly car part. We ran all around Forest View, up and down every street, calling "Star! Star!" We asked everyone we passed if they'd seen him. No one had.

We even walked around the edges of Forest View, in case he'd left the trailer park. Most of the yards backed up to a tall chain-link fence with a bunch of gigantic pipes on the other side. We followed the fence and got to a small highway, where cars whizzed by. Then we walked along the edge of the highway and through the backyards of two run-down hotels. And then we were back at the chain-link fence and the giant pipes.

"I wish we took a picture of him," Crystal said. "Then we could photocopy it and put up signs all over the telephone poles."

I thought about that. "But what if his owner saw it and got mad?"

Crystal shrugged. "Well, maybe we could call the pound and see if Star's there."

"We can't."

"Why not?"

"We don't have papers or tags or anything to prove it. Plus, we're under eighteen."

Plus, I thought secretly, what if the pound people found out I didn't have papers, either? What if my whole family got *deportada* because of me?

Our legs were tired by now. And we were shivery cold because the sun was going down and the wind was picking up. Even so, we went back to the forest in case Star had come back.

He hadn't.

So we sat in his spot and cried together.

"Maybe he just went exploring for a little while," I said, when I was ready to stop sniffling.

Crystal nodded. "Maybe he'll be back tomorrow."

By the time we came out of the forest, it was dark. We walked fast by the broken-glass park. There were already guys hanging out there, smoking and drinking beer and talking loud. Luckily they didn't notice Crystal and me.

When I got home, Mamá grabbed me and hugged me so tight I could barely breathe.

"*Dios*, Zitlally, where were you?"

"With Crystal," I said.

"Are you all right?"

She probably saw my red eyes and blotchy face and the crusty stuff around my eyes.

"Something sad happened." And I thought, *I'll just tell her about Star and maybe she can help us get him back so he can do his tricks for Papá.* But when I opened my mouth to tell her, I noticed her face.

Something was wrong, something more than me coming home late. Her face was like mine—blotchy and crusty. Her eyes were red, too.

She didn't ask me what sad thing had happened. Instead, she said, "Zitlally, we have bad news, *mi amor.*"

Behind her, Reina and Dalia were hugging each other on the sofa. They looked like someone had just died. Was it Star? Was he hit by a car? Did they somehow know he was mine?

"It's your father, *mi vida.* He's *secuestrado.*"

I thought I knew what *secuestrado* meant, but maybe I didn't, because it only happened in movies, not in real life.

But then I knew I was right, because Dalia said, in English, "Kidnapped."

Secuestrado, secuestrado, secuestrado.

All night, that was all Mamá talked about, on the phone with my aunts Rosa and Virginia and María. With Uncle Luciano in Mexico. And when she said *secuestrado*, she was always tugging at her hair, or twisting her rings, or wringing a dishtowel. And she was shaking, like when the cop pulled her over, only that lasted five minutes, and this was lasting much, much longer.

Mamá said that some bad men had called her that afternoon. They were holding Papá prisoner in the desert. They wouldn't let him go until she paid them ten thousand dollars. She told them she didn't have that much money. They said, "Find it," and hung up.

We didn't sleep. We stayed up all night and whispered to each other, *secuestrado, secuestrado, secuestrado.* We said the names of the entire Holy

Family over and over again. *Jesús María José Jesús María José Jesús María José.*

Saturday morning, Crystal came to the door and said, "Want to look for Star?"

I shook my head.

"Oh." She peered over my shoulder. "Is your dad here?"

"No. There's a problem." I looked down at my furry slippers. "Anyway, I can't talk now."

She seemed hurt, but I closed the screen door and went back to the bedroom with Reina and Dalia and watched TV all weekend.

But I didn't actually watch TV. I stared at the moving shapes and colors and wondered how it felt to be *secuestrado.* I wondered if they were giving Papá food. I wondered if he was blindfolded.

On Monday and Tuesday I didn't go to school and Mamá didn't notice.

Crystal did.

She left the notes and handouts and homework assignments at my door in big yellow envelopes covered in glittery dolphin stickers. She'd re-copied all her notes onto pink notebook paper for me. She had neat bubbly handwriting, and over each of her *i*'s she made tiny dog faces. It looked like a lot of work.

I asked Mamá how it felt to be *secuestrado* and if Papá had food and if he was blindfolded.

She didn't want to answer. She said I'd have nightmares.

So I asked Dalia what had happened to Papá. Exactly.

She told me. She said that there are bad men who roam the desert at the border. They look like ranchers, and they drive their trucks around and if they see *migrantes* who look thirsty and hungry and lost, they say, *Get in the back of the truck and we'll give you sandwiches and Coke*. And even if you have a bad feeling in your stomach about it, you get in because they have pistols in their jeans. And then they take you to their house and lock you in a room with no windows and call your family and say if they don't get money wired to them soon, they'll kill you. Dalia knows this because it happened to her old boyfriend when he crossed.

"Is Papá blindfolded?" Somehow being blindfolded seemed like it would be the worst part. Not being able to see. Not knowing what was happening. Or what would happen next.

"Who knows." Dalia thought. "I bet he's just locked in a room."

"With food?"

"I bet they give him food." Usually Dalia didn't like to answer my questions, but now she was patient. "But probably it's bad food, like old tortillas and cold, crusty beans without salsa."

"Maybe Mamá could call the police," I said.

"She can't. Because we have no idea where Papá is. And he's illegal. No one cares about him but us. And if the cops found him, they'd send him back to Mexico again."

I took a warm bath with lots of bubbles and

closed my eyes and imagined I was in a dark room with bad food. And then I tried to imagine where Star was—probably in a dark place, too, probably scared and hungry and missing me. It was true, their fates were all tied up together.

Way back, before we left Mexico, Papá knew everything and could do anything. When I was six, on the day before we left for Colorado, we went on a picnic in Xono. "Pay attention to every-thing, *m'hija*," he said. "Because we might not be back for a long, long time." He rubbed his hand over his face and Mamá touched his shoulder.

We found a spot by the stream on wispy, light green grass. I paid attention to how soft it was, like a mat of feathers. I paid attention to how the trickling water rang light as bird songs in some places and deep as church bells in others.

Papá found a spot where the stream poured straight out of some mossy stones. He filled a cup and let Dalia and Mamá and me take turns drinking the cold, sweet water. *How does he know,* I wondered, *which water makes you sick and which water is good?*

I wolfed down my lunch so I could play in the stream with Dalia. When I hopped to my feet, Papá held up a tiny piece of my leftover avocado-and-cheese sandwich. "Are you going to finish?"

I shook my head and splashed into the water.

He smiled sideways. "This bit of sandwich could be a feast for forty-seven ants."

I stopped splashing. "Really? How many would it take to eat a whole sandwich?"

He looked at the sky and thought. "Five hundred sixty-two." He tossed the sandwich scrap into the trees, and I imagined hundreds of ants pouncing on it. Then he winked at me. "But only five hundred thirty-three if they're really hungry."

How does Papá know this? I thought. *Is there anything he doesn't know?*

Then we came to Colorado. And here, every day I found out new things he didn't know and couldn't do. He couldn't ask the lady at Walmart where the garbage bags were. He couldn't pronounce the name of my school. He didn't know about the silent *e* rule. He probably didn't even know how many American ants it took to eat one sandwich.

Sometimes I liked being the expert. I felt proud explaining that in English, *j* makes a *j* sound, not an *h* sound. Or asking the guy at Ace Hardware if the fifty-percent-off Christmas lights were already marked down. Or reading the sign over the pink ice cream, which said it was peppermint, not strawberry.

But sometimes I wished we could go back to the day of the picnic by the stream, when Papá knew everything and could do anything. Back to a time when I'd never heard of *deportado* or *secuestrado*. Back then, I would never, ever—not in a million years—have imagined that these things could happen to Papá.

On Wednesday, I went to school. It distracted me a little from imagining Papá locked in a dark room with bad food.

Crystal was extra nice to me. "Your hair looks pretty," she said, even though it was the same as always.

"You didn't find Star, did you?" I asked.

She shook her head. "I left a bunch of bologna there, but I think the squirrels just ate it."

At lunch, over mushy cafeteria pizza, she explained how to add and subtract fractions, since I'd missed it in math class. On her napkin, she drew a picture of a pizza with ten pieces. "That's ten tenths," she began. "And each of these pieces is one tenth."

After she finished, I thought of the $10,000 Mamá needed as one pizza. She had $5,000 left from selling Papá's truck, which was $5,000/$10,000, like half the pizza. And she had $1,000 saved in the bank, which was like one piece of pizza. So she had to beg all her friends and relatives and people she worked with for $4,000 more, which was like four slices of pizza. Problem was, each of her friends only had a little bite-sized piece of pizza. This meant she was on the phone all the time, searching for the four-tenths she needed, saying *secuestrado*, *secuestrado*, *secuestrado*.

The word had started hurting, like a little needle, stabbing me. I didn't want to go home and have to hear it again all afternoon. "Want to go to the forest today?" I asked Crystal.

"Yeah," she said. She made her voice low and serious. "Zitlally, we need to make a plan."

· 9 ·

In the forest, we leaned against the tires of the truck, with our heads back and eyes closed and mouths open. The sun was shining onto our faces, straight into our mouths.

We were eating sunshine.

That was Crystal's idea. She said that when she was little and there wasn't any food in the house, she'd go outside and eat sunshine. She'd find patches of it shining through tree leaves and lick it up with her finger. It always made her feel better.

That's what we were doing in the car part forest, trying to feel better.

Crystal smacked her lips. "Yum." Then she said, "Zitlally. Where's your dad?"

I thought about saying Antarctica or Madagascar. But I couldn't think of another country that fast, and if I said Antarctica or Madagascar, she'd know I was copying. Anyway, why lie? Even if she told other people about Papá, they'd figure she was lying. But really, I didn't think she'd tell anyone.

"He's kidnapped."

"Oh my God!" Crystal said.

And I spilled out the whole story, even the part about how he didn't have papers. I tried to end on a positive note. "We don't think they blindfolded him, at least."

"Well, that's good, I guess." She sat quiet for a minute, thinking, and I could practically see the thoughts firing off like comets in her head. She was smart, I realized. The way she'd explained fractions at lunch, even better than our math teacher could do—that's what made me realize how smart she was. There was a whole galaxy of smart thoughts in her brain, all lit up like stars.

Suddenly, her head snapped up and she said, "That's it!"

"What?"

Her eyes were blazing, like a meteor shower was happening behind them. "Guess who your dad's spirit animal is, Zit?"

For a second I didn't say anything. Then, quietly, I said, "Star."

"Exactly. Right when Star went missing, your dad went missing."

Of course, I'd known this all along, but now that Crystal said it out loud, I knew what I had to do. "If I get Star back, my dad will come home."

Crystal patted my shoulder. "I'll help you find him."

"Thanks," I said, and she kept patting my shoulder.

"It's my duty as your best friend," she said. She rested her hand on my back. "Plus, your dad's life depends on it."

Our plan was to knock on the door of every single trailer in Forest View and ask if they knew anything about Star. There were two hundred trailers total. We knew this because each one was numbered, black numbers on a white sign over the door, except for some trailers where it had fallen off and no one bothered to put it back up. We decided to do forty trailers per day, or one-fifth.

So, in five days or sooner, we'd find Star. Or at least information leading to Star.

I just hoped Papá could hold out for that long.

It's amazing how many different kinds of people there are in this world, even in this trailer park.

Some people were nice, and smiled sadly when

we asked about Star, and said they'd pray for him. One lady offered us a puppy to take Star's place, but we said no thanks. It was Star we wanted, not any other dog in the world besides Star.

Some people didn't open the screen door. They looked up from the TV and called out "What?!" And when we asked about Star, they grunted "No." Some people acted like we were dumb because we didn't know Star's breed and he didn't have tags.

Crystal talked most of the time, and I hung back, feeling shy. "Hi!" she'd say. "I'm Crystal and this is my best friend, Zitlally. . . ."

In about one-third of the houses, no one spoke English, so I had to speak Spanish. After the first one, Crystal said, "Wow! You're smart! You speak two languages perfectly!"

I'd never thought about it that way before. I liked thinking about it that way. I especially liked thinking, *Wow, Mamá's smart. She speaks two languages, and even if her English isn't perfect, she still speaks two, which is more than most people. And Papá speaks three!*

For three days, we went from house to house, carrying a notebook to mark off which houses we'd been to, and also to write down clues. But no one knew anything. Our page titled *Notes* was blank.

Meanwhile, over those days, Mamá collected the $4,000 she needed in bits and pieces. On the fourth day, Saturday, she went to send the money from the Tienda Mexicana just outside Forest View. I didn't go with her because I didn't want to get behind on our forty trailers per day. And good thing I didn't, because on the fourth day, something happened.

In trailer #142, a little kid, maybe four years old, with wild black hair, answered the door.

"Is your mom or dad here?" Crystal asked.

He stared.

I asked him in Spanish.

He shook his head.

"Any grown-ups or big kids?" I asked in Spanish.

He nodded. "But Nora's asleep."

After I translated, Crystal bent down to his level and looked him straight in the eyes. "Have you seen a well-trained, fit, handsome white dog about this tall with a beautiful black star on the back of his neck?" Then she said to me, out of the corner of her mouth, "Ask him in Spanish, Zit."

I did, except I didn't know how to say *well-trained* or *fit,* so I skipped those parts.

The boy said, "A long time ago. When it was still cold."

"Where?" I said.

He pointed to the trailer next door, #143. "Mr. Ed got a dog but it kept digging holes everywhere and my mom said she was calling the dog police to take him away."

"And then?" I asked.

"And then the dog was gone."

When I explained everything to Crystal, her eyes got big. "Could be Star," she said.

"Could be," I agreed.

We thanked the boy and went to trailer #143.

We rang the doorbell.

No answer.

We knocked.

No answer.

We pounded with our fists.

No answer.

We peered through the window. It was dirty and the blinds were down but we saw a sliver of a very messy living room, packed with furniture and boxes and magazines and junk. No sign of Star.

Beside the trailer, in a patch of gravel, was a lopsided truck with a falling-off bumper. Lacy bits of brown rust peeked through the orange paint. This truck would have fit right into the car part forest.

Behind the truck was a small, scrappy yard, mostly mud and dirt with some grass around the edges. Sad-looking, forgotten-looking junk was piled up against the side of the trailer—an old refrigerator and a vacuum cleaner and a toaster oven. And at the back sat a little shed, with peeling red paint and the roof half caved in.

"Listen!" Crystal said.

I listened.

The faintest sound came from the shed, a high whine. A whimper. An animal in pain.

I creaked open the metal gate and walked to the shed. Crystal followed. We creeped around it. The whimpering was louder now. There were no windows, only a door with an open padlock.

"Should we open it?" I asked.

"We have to," said Crystal.

And she took my hand in hers and I squeezed it, hard, and with my other hand I opened the door, just a little, just enough to see in. A thin line of light came through the door and lit up Star.

"Star!" Crystal shouted.

"Star!" I shouted.

For a long time we hugged him. He stopped whimpering and licked us all over our faces and up and down our arms. And then, our eyes got used to the darkness, and we saw that Star was hurt.

There was a torn-up strip of a blue flannel shirt tied around his front leg, right where the leg met his body. Silver duct tape was wrapped over the flannel. The shirt was dirty and stained with blood. Some of the blood looked old and brown and dried. Some looked fresh and red and new. And it stank so much it covered up Star's naturally good dog smell.

His nose was dry and he seemed thirsty, but the bowl beside him was empty.

"He's been kidnapped," Crystal said solemnly.

"*Secuestrado,*" I whispered to myself. And then, more loudly, I said, "Let's get him out of here." The place was creepy, full of old, broken machines, lawn mowers and Weedwackers and chain saws and tools and wheelbarrows. Toward the back were bags of dirt and bottles of weed poisons and stacks of old plastic boxes and fishing rods. It smelled like old metal mixed with dirt and chemicals.

"Think he can walk okay?" Crystal asked.

"He has to," I said. "At least three-fourths of his legs work okay. He can do it. He's strong. He's Star."

"We better hurry," Crystal said. "His evil kidnapper could be back any minute now."

And that's when the door swung open and daylight blinded me.

I blinked a few times, and then I saw him, the evil kidnapper, looming over us, holding a pointy-tipped cane above his head.

· 10 ·

He was old, maybe seventy, and his hair was white
and clipped close to his skull and his face was all
wrinkles and brown age spots and big ugly moles
and warts and black dots and heavy bags pulling
down his eyes. His fingernails were like yellow
claws clamped around the cane. He was skinny,
with a flannel shirt hanging from his bones, like
the one around Star's leg, only his was red and

black with a holey T-shirt underneath, and little white hairs poking out the neckline. He hardly had lips, just two tiny slivers of chappedness a shade darker than his pasty skin, and bubbles of spit at the corners.

He lowered his cane.

Crystal stood up and held out her hand. "You must be Mr. Ed."

"Speak up, child," he said. "These ears ain't what they used to be." His words creaked out like he was an old machine himself, like his voice was something that needed to be oiled.

Crystal shouted, "YOU MUST BE MR. ED!"

"Indeed I am, child, indeed I am." He coughed a few times without covering his mouth. Then he said, "What are you gals doing in my shed?"

I thought this would be a good time to run for it, because who knew if he'd start bashing us with his cane? But that would mean abandoning Star, which I just couldn't do.

Crystal yelled, "YOU HAVE OUR DOG!"

Mr. Ed chuckled, and you could see his teeth,

which were stained all shades of yellow and brown, crooked, some missing, about one-fifth. "You gals been the ones feeding him down there in that old junkyard?"

I felt offended that he called our forest a junkyard. Especially considering what his own house looked like.

But Crystal just nodded.

"Well, then I owe you some thanks, gals."

Crystal and I looked at each other.

"And good thing you came when you did. Say yer goodbyes. I'm just about to take him to the pound."

"OVER OUR DEAD BODIES!" Crystal screamed, throwing her arms around Star.

"Now, calm yerself down, child."

"WHAT DID YOU DO TO HIM?" Crystal demanded.

He coughed a few more times and put down his cane and sat on a stump by the shed door. Then he laid the cane across his lap and told us the story of how he got Star, who he called Jim-Boy.

"This past winter, one nice, warm day, I'm fishing up the Poudre River, and I find a dirty, skinny dog on the roadside. He sits next to me real nice, and I say to myself, he'll make a fine fishing companion. So I take him home and then he starts with this digging. Digging holes everywhere, and then the neighbors start their bellyaching. 'Oh, he's messing up my garden! Oh, I'm calling the dog cops!' So I tie him up in that junkyard, thinking he's just digging 'cause he's bored, and come spring, when we go fishing every day, he'll stop. Why is it that dogs are always digging? Like them squirrels. I put bird seeds out for the birds, but them squirrels gobble it right up, the rascals."

I was wondering what birdseed and squirrels had to do with Star, when Mr. Ed looked at his cane, all muddled, and said, "Now, what was I saying?"

"You're talking about Star," Crystal said.

"What's that?"

"STAR!" Crystal shouted. "WHY YOU TIED HIM UP AND LEFT HIM FOR DEAD."

"Oh, yeah. Well, wouldn't you know it, day after I tie him up, I fall and break my hip. In the hospital for weeks. I tell my nurses, I say, there's a dog in the junkyard that's wanting water and food pretty bad. And they think I'm crazy and tell me, 'Now, sir, you just rest up and eat and watch TV and get yerself better.' And I was happy there, with the good food, and all those channels. They got cable, you know. And you know what they say about hospital food tasting like cardboard? Not true! Every morning, oatmeal. Coffee. Juice. That fancy green fruit, what's that called—honey something—"

Crystal stood up, like the fancy green fruit was the straw that broke the camel's back. "STAR! STAR! WHAT HAPPENED WITH STAR?!"

"I'm just getting to that, missy. I come back from the hospital last week, and I'm thinking I got to go find that dog and bury him. But I'll be dog-goned, he's alive. So I say, Jim-Boy, it's a pretty day, and you and me are going fishing! I put him in the back of my old pickup and we head out. But we're on that Poudre Canyon road, going fast, when he gets it in his pea brain to jump out. I pull over, and I'm thinking he's a goner, but he's laying there whining.

"So I bring him home and put him in the shed. No money to take him to the dog doctor. But every day it's worse, and that shoulder's smelling bad now, so I got no choice but the pound. Make matters worse, my daughter says I'm moving in with her. Says I'm incompetent or some such thing. Says I got no business having a dog if I can't hardly take care of myself. Won't let me drive no more, neither. Look, here Jenny comes now."

And at that moment, a little two-door car screeched to a stop next to Mr. Ed's truck. Like a fast, mean dust storm, Jenny jumped out.

Jenny's face was twisted into a frown. Maybe it got stuck that way and she didn't know how to unstick it. Maybe her frown had something to do with her hair, which was frizzy, like it had gotten tangled up in Velcro. Her black jeans and gray T-shirt matched the shadows under her eyes. Sharp elbows jutted out from her waist in angry little triangles.

She looked at me and Crystal and her frown got deeper, but she didn't say anything to us. She just waved her hand in front of her nose and said, "Pee-*yooo*, that dog smells bad."

Right away I thought, *Now, she's someone I would* not *want to be best friends with*. And I felt extra-appreciative of Crystal.

"Come on, Dad," Jenny said. She grabbed his arm and pushed his cane into his hand. Then she frowned at Star. "How are we gonna get it into the truck, I'd like to know?"

Crystal clamped her arms around Star and said, like she was queen of the universe, "We'll be taking Star."

Jenny furrowed her eyebrows. "Star?"

"He's not It," Crystal said. "He's Star."

"Go on home, girls." Jenny waved us away, while Mr. Ed stayed quiet at her side. "I got to do this," she said. "Not exactly a fun thing, taking a dog to meet his end."

"What?!" I heard myself scream.

"You think they got medicine to waste on a full-grown dog? No, they'll put him right out of his misery."

I threw myself on Star and hung on. He whimpered, but I'm sure that inside he was glad we were protecting him.

Jenny leaned against the wall, blew her bangs out of her eyes. "Your parents want a dog? You got the money for his vet bills?"

Crystal stuck out her chin. "Of course. My father's a vet. We have a giant fenced-in yard and a state-of-the-art doghouse. It's dog paradise. Actually, we were in the market for a dog, a big white one, as a matter of fact. Well trained and fit and handsome."

Jenny narrowed her eyes. The black eyeliner around the edges made her look a little like a frizzly-haired vampire. I hugged Star tighter.

"Fine," she said after a while. "Take him. But if this so-called vet father of yours says you can't keep him, don't bring him back here."

Mr. Ed gave Star a pat on the head and then let Jenny drag him toward the trailer by the elbow. He called over his shoulder, "You gals take him on home in that there wheelbarrow. Keep it. Lord knows I won't be wheeling nothing around myself anymore. Take care of old Jim-Boy. He's a good dog."

"THANKS, MR. ED!" we said, and started heaving Star into the wheelbarrow.

On the way home Crystal said, "I don't hate Mr. Ed. Not exactly."

"Yeah, he's not an evil kidnapper after all."

"He reminds me of my grandpa a little," she said.

It was hard to hear her over the squeaky wheels, which sounded like a herd of dying elephants.

In Crystal's trailer, we could hear yelling.

"The dictator's back?" I said.

"He's back," she sighed.

So we wheeled Star to my trailer instead. Mamá didn't like dogs, and I had a feeling she wouldn't be happy to have Star stay with us in the middle of a catastrophe.

But Mamá wasn't home, just Dalia and Reina, watching TV. Mamá was probably still wiring the money.

I left Crystal and Star outside our door and stood in front of the TV so my sisters had to pay attention to me. "*Hermanas*, there's something you need to see."

They followed me outside, and I introduced them to Star. He was sitting in the wheelbarrow, and he offered them a handshake with the paw of his good leg. You could practically see their hearts melting, even though his shoulder was stinky. I explained to them how I found Star and how we fed him and trained him and then how he got hurt and was stuck in Mr. Ed's dark shed with no windows for days.

"So you had a secret dog all this time?" Dalia said. "That's where you always disappear to?"

I nodded.

Crystal said, "Star's in trouble. We need to get him to a vet."

"You got money for a vet?" Dalia asked Crystal. She shook her head.

"Well, neither do we," Dalia said. "Like not even five dollars for groceries."

I was a little embarrassed she said this to Crystal. But it was true. Yesterday we had to go to the food bank, and even though the food wasn't bad—the little plastic cups of frozen peaches were actually pretty tasty—still, it was the *food bank*. It was worse than getting your clothes at garage sales.

"Money doesn't matter," Crystal said. "We'll bring Star to the vet and figure out how to pay later."

I gave Star water and fried him bacon while Dalia looked in the phone book and found the closest vet. It was about a mile away. We wheelbarrowed Star through Forest View, out to the highway, and followed the highway past the run-down hotels and Mexican grocery stores. We fed him bits of bacon along the way to keep up his spirits.

Even though Dalia didn't like to walk, and didn't like to be seen with kids, she only complained once, after a big blue truck blasting *rancheras* drove by. She muttered, "None of my friends better see me pushing this dog around with you two."

Reina was a trouper, too. She had to walk twice as fast as us on her chubby little legs to keep up, but she only made us carry her for a couple of minutes.

After a half hour or so, we reached a pink cement building that said HAPPY PET VETERINARY CLINIC with a picture of a cartoon dog on one side and a cartoon cat on the other and a small sign underneath that said SE HABLA ESPAÑOL.

Crystal whispered, "Zitlally, we have to convince them to help Star. Remember, whatever happens to Star happens to your dad."

When Crystal said that, all the quiet, scared tears inside me turned into words, a whole giant ocean of words, wave after wave after wave of words. And I knew just what I had to do with them.

· 11 ·

I marched straight to the counter and locked eyes with a lady with black-and-orange-striped hair. In Spanish, I said, "*Señora*, we found Star and took care of him, but then he fell out of a truck and hurt his leg. We don't have papers or tags or anything, and we don't even know if he got his shots. But we love him and we give him bacon and we trained him to sit in a truck and beep a horn and we pushed him all the way here in a wheelbarrow. We don't have money to pay you. But it's very, very important that you save him. And Crystal and me will do anything. We'll sell lemonade all summer and bring you all the money we make. We'll work for you and clean up dog fur and cat poop or anything you want. *Por favor, señora, por favor.*"

Crystal's mouth was practically hanging open at my speech, even though she didn't understand a word except *Star*.

The lady said in Spanish, "*Señorita*, this dog is lucky to have you. We'll do everything we can for him."

The vet was another nice lady who wore a light blue doctor's coat and spoke Spanish, too. While she examined Star, she let us stay in the room and put our hands on his fur to calm him. She cleaned his wound and put an antiseptic on it and complimented us on how well-behaved he was when he shook her hand. She gave him the shots he needed, and he barely winced because we fed him bits of bacon and petted him the whole time. Then she handed us a rabies tag and a collar and told us to come back after he was better to get him neutered, and they'd figure out a way to pay for it if we couldn't.

She even gave us a little bottle of antibiotic pills to give him for ten days straight. And I knew that if he didn't want to take them, we could just dissolve them with a little Coke and have him lap it up.

On the way home, Star seemed better already, although maybe it was just all that bacon sitting happy in his belly.

"Your speech worked miracles!" Crystal kept saying. "Zit, you're something else!"

Back at home, Crystal went into her trailer, and Star came into mine. Mamá was home by then, and once Dalia and Reina and I explained everything about Star, she said he could stay inside the house just until he got better, but after that he'd have to stay outside. I hugged Mamá and she hugged me back and whispered, "Let's hope

119

they let your father go, Zitlally. I don't know what I'll do if they don't let him go."

I looked at Star, all cozy on an old blanket beside the sofa. "I have a feeling he'll be okay, Mamá."

Sunday morning before church, Star was chomping on bacon from a bowl at my feet, and I was eating hotcakes with lots of syrup, when the phone rang. The phone didn't usually ring so early, so I thought it must be either really good news or really bad news. I picked it up.

And heard Papá's voice.

"Zitlally!" And then he spoke in star language, all *husssshhhhh*es and whispers, telling me how much he loved me.

"Are you free, Papá?"

"Yes, *m'hija*. I'm free."

I wanted to shout as loud as I could "WOOOHOOO!!!" and tell Mamá, who was in the shower, and Reina, who was still asleep, and

Dalia, who was putting on makeup in the bed-room. But more than that, I wanted him all to my-self for a minute. "What happened, Papá?"

"Well, *m'hija*, after they got the money, they put me in the back of a pickup truck and said they'd take me to the bus stop. But I had a feeling they were lying. I had a feeling they were drop-ping me off for *la migra* to get me. So I jumped out of the truck and rolled down a ditch. I hurt my shoulder on a rock when I hit the ground, but I got up and ran down the canyon. I ran faster than ever before."

"As fast as a dog?" I asked.

"Yes, *m'hija*, as fast as a dog. And I found my way to the bus stop, and here I am in Arizona, and I'm catching the next bus to Colorado."

"Do you have money, Papá?"

"I taped a hundred dollars to my leg before I left. I'll be there by tomorrow night, *m'hija*."

And then Mamá came out of the bathroom, asking who I was talking to, and I said, "Papá," with the biggest smile in the galaxy on my face. And she was screaming and then Dalia came out waving her mascara wand and screaming, and then Reina woke up and started screaming and we were all screaming and dancing and hugging each other.

· 12 ·

At school on Monday, I could not stop smiling. When Mr. Martin asked what two-sevenths times three was, I raised my hand high and proud like a flag and said, "Six-sevenths!" I felt bright, like that sunshine I ate was shooting out all over the place.

Emma and Olivia and Morgan must have noticed this and decided I wasn't boring anymore, because Morgan asked if I wanted to go bike riding with them in the park after school. It was lunchtime, and we were in the bathroom, and they were putting on lip gloss and brushing their hair, and I was washing my hands, and Crystal was in the bathroom stall. I could feel her listening.

"Thanks, Morgan, but Crystal and me have plans. Maybe another time."

Later, after school, Crystal said, "Zit, do we really have plans?"

"Of course! My dad will be home by tonight. We have to practice Star's dog show!"

We wheelbarrowed Star down the path. It was warm enough for shorts and tank tops, and my legs and arms felt happy and free and soaking up sunshine. The air smelled sweet, like nectar and grass and trees. Tiny flowers had popped up next to the fallen tulips and daffodils. The petals were in a perfect, cheerful circle, blue around a yellow center.

"Forget-me-nots!" Crystal said.

"What?"

"Those flowers. That's what they're called. It's like nature put them there 'cause it knew your dad was coming home!"

I picked some blossoms and stuck them in Star's collar so he'd look extra *guapo* for Papá.

"Crystal," I said. "I've been thinking about something." And I had, all night. I'd hardly slept, thinking about Papá and Star and how happy I was, but then, when I thought of Crystal, I felt a little sad. I'd get my dad back, but hers was still in jail.

"What?" she said.

"I think you should keep Star."

Her face lit up. "Really?"

I nodded. "But we can bring him here every day and hang out. And if the dictator's in a bad mood, you and Star can come over to my house. And if you have to go to Madagascar to visit your dad, we can watch Star."

"I'll treat him like gold, Zit, I promise!"

In the forest, we helped Star out of the wheelbarrow. His leg was looking good, getting better fast. He walked with just a small limp back to his old spot under the rusty rainbow truck hood.

"Sit, Star," Crystal said.

Star sat.

"Shake, Star," I said.

Star shook my hand.

"Roll over, Star," Crystal said.

Star rolled over.

Then, together, we helped him into the driver's seat of the truck. He sat there with his tongue hanging out, pink and happy. I said, "Beep!"

He put his good paw on the horn and beeped and beeped and beeped.

Then he stopped and his ears moved up, alert and listening. He was looking at something past our heads, behind us.

I turned around, and there he was. Papá.

Laughing and laughing. Laughing so hard he was nearly peeing in his pants.

I ran to him and he held me tight, and it was just how I'd imagined, me burying my face in his T-shirt. He whispered in star language in my ear, "*Ni-mitz nequi.*" I love you. Over and over and over again.

Then he looked at Star and said, "*¡Que perro!*" What a dog!

"His name is Star," I said.

I hugged Papá again, as tight as I could.

"Careful, *m'hija*. My shoulder's pretty sore." He pulled aside his T-shirt neck and showed me a big white bandage taped to his shoulder.

"I have a feeling it'll get better fast," I said.

Crystal had helped Star out of the truck and was sitting next to him, petting him, looking sad and happy at once. I felt like hugging her, too.

Crystal said, "*Mucho gusto*, Mr. Mora. I'm Crystal."

127

"*Mucho gusto*, Crystal."

"I was practicing my *mucho gusto*s for a while," she said. "Zit told me you'd be coming home, so I figured out how to say 'Nice to meet you,' and now I finally get to say it to you. Did I say it right?"

"Perfectly," Papá said.

Crystal nudged Star toward Papá. "Star, meet Mr. Mora." She whispered to Papá, "Hold out your hand."

Papá held out his hand.

Star shook it.

Papá laughed some more, and then he looked closely at Crystal. "You're the girl who lives next door, right?"

She nodded. "With my mother, and sometimes her boyfriend. He's not my dad, though." She kept petting Star. "My dad's in jail. He'll be out in seven years if he's on good behavior. And he will be on good behavior because he's good. And he loves me more than anything and wants to come home to me. He's a good dad."

I stared at Crystal. Her eyes looked real, like

when Dalia takes off all her makeup at night and you can see her skin all tender underneath.

Papá said to Crystal, "I'm sure he has a good heart. His daughter does." He smiled, and his front tooth lined with gold flashed in the sunshine.

"*Vámonos*," he said. "Your mother and sisters are waiting for us. They have a surprise." He reached his hand out to Crystal. "Of course, you're invited, too, Crystal."

We walked back together, taking turns wheelbarrowing Star, through the forget-me-nots and summery air, back to our trailer, where a dazzling white cake was waiting for us. *Bienvenido Papá y Feliz Cumpleaños Zitlally!* Welcome Papá and Happy Birthday Zitlally! This time all the *l*'s were there, like brilliant blue pieces of sky over white Antarctic snow.

The Deepest, Most Magical Forest

This happened a long, long time ago, Zitlally. It happened to the grandfather of my grandfather. Or maybe even his grandfather.

One night, when he was a tiny baby, his mother wrapped him in three blankets and laid him in a clearing in the deepest, most magical forest.

The forest where one must never cut firewood because of the tree spirits.

Where one must never pick berries because of the plant spirits.

Where one must never hunt because of the animal spirits.

But this baby's mother was special. She was a

healer. She asked the spirits permission to enter the forest, so they let her gather healing herbs. Always, she thanked them. Tonight, she had come to discover her child's spirit animal. She stayed hidden in the trees, watching, waiting for her son's creature to come.

At dawn, a dove landed near the baby's head. His mother thought, *Maybe his animal is a bird. Then he can fly over his troubles!* But the dove moved on.

Then a small lizard crept near the baby's feet. *Maybe his animal is a lizard*, thought his mother. *Then he will be stealthy and agile!* But the lizard moved on.

And then, just as the sun peeked over the mountaintops, a young deer wobbled into the clearing. Slowly, step by step, the fawn walked to the baby. For a long time, the fawn looked into the baby's eyes.

The baby looked back.

The fawn's long tongue reached out and licked the baby's face.

The baby smiled.

The fawn smiled.

Finally, the fawn walked away. That was when the baby's mother noticed the pattern of white spots on the fawn's back, how it echoed the odd birthmark on her son's back. She picked him up and kissed him and whispered thanks and headed home. She smiled the whole way, happy that her son's spirit animal was the swiftest, most graceful, most noble creature of the forest.

Sure enough, the baby grew into a boy who could out-run anyone, even the fastest man. When he ran up-hill, it was as though he was running downhill. When he ran downhill, it was as though he was flying. But since he was the best at running, the boy wanted to be the best at everything. The best tree climber, the best whistler, the best hunter.

There was a problem with being the best hunter. His older brothers wouldn't even let him touch their rifles. "You're too little," they said when they left to go hunting.

They made him stay home to help his mother. Patients came all day long, and she cured them with herbs. The boy felt bored helping her. He whined, "I want to hunt and show the world that I'm the best at everything."

"It's true, you're a good runner," she said. "But that's thanks to your deer spirit. You must always be grateful for this gift."

But the boy did not feel grateful. He felt only proud of himself. "I run fast because I'm fast," he said. "And if my brothers let me hunt, I'd be the best hunter and then you'd see."

"Hmph," his mother said, and went back to hanging up her herbs to dry.

Very early one morning, while the stars were still out, even before his mother had woken up to start the tortillas and tea, the boy tiptoed outside with his oldest brother's rifle. He shivered in the darkness and put the heavy gun over his shoulder and walked over the hills and through the fields, headed straight for the deepest, most magical forest.

The forest where one must never cut firewood because of the tree spirits.

Where one must never pick berries because of the plant spirits.

Where, most of all, one must never hunt because of the animal spirits.

The boy went there anyway. It was the only place where no one would see him. No one would see him because no one was brave enough to venture there.

He thought, *I am the best and the bravest*, and just as the sky was turning from the black of night to the blue of morning, he stepped into the deepest, most magical forest.

Here the trees whispered, the plants murmured, the insects sang. If he'd listened carefully, he would have heard the warnings in their words. *You foolish boy! Leave, leave, leave! Or else!*

But he didn't listen. He crept through the underbrush, thinking, *I'm about to become the best hunter this pueblo has ever seen.*

The boy sat down and waited by a big tree at the edge of a clearing. After a while, he heard a movement. Into the meadow stepped a magnificent buck. It held its head high, and its antlers came to four points on each side, like a majestic crown. If the boy had looked closely, he might have noticed the animal's pattern of white spots, how it matched the strange birthmark on his own back.

But he didn't notice.

The boy stood up slowly, thinking about how big and impressed his brothers' eyes would be when they saw him carrying this giant animal's head. He raised the gun to his shoulder, moved his eye to the sight, and pulled the trigger.

So many things happened in that one terrible moment.

The entire forest shook like thunder.

The deer flew back in the air and landed with its legs collapsed beneath it.

135

And the force from the gunshot launched the boy backward. He landed on something sharp, something that stabbed through his thigh. A spiked branch poking from a log like a knife.

The buck limped away, blood streaming from its leg. The boy tried to stand up, but his leg didn't support him. It ached and burned. Blood gushed from the wound. He left the gun there and dragged himself toward home, crawling most of the way.

Hours later, he made it to the kitchen door. His mother scooped him up and brought him inside. She cleaned his wound as he screamed in pain.

"It pierced you to the bone," she said. "How did this happen, son?"

"I woke up early to gather firewood," he lied. "And I tripped and fell."

She raised an eyebrow but said nothing.

Two days later, the boy's wound was worse, pink and swollen, with red streaks running up and down his leg. He lay on his mat and shivered and sweated with fever. All night and all day, his mother had been tending to him with her worried face.

That afternoon, his brother said, "Where's my gun? It's been missing for two days."

Their mother gave her wounded son a look full of questions.

When the boy told her the truth, his words sounded faraway, as though they came from another boy's mouth. That was how lost he was in fever and pain.

"You shot a deer in the magical forest?" his mother cried. She leapt up and threw food and blankets and pots and cups and herbs and matches into a bag. She hoisted her son onto her back and strapped him on with rope like a bundle of firewood. Then she headed to the deepest, most magical forest. Every step, every bounce sent more fire through the boy's leg, but he only whimpered. He was beyond words now, beyond crying. He drifted in and out of this world, so close to death.

Inside the forest, the light was different. It was golden and spilled in ribbons through the leaves. Golden ribbons pooled on the forest floor. The boy wanted to let one of the golden ribbons pull him up and up and into heaven.

But then his mother was pouring cold water on his face and saying, "Where? Where did you shoot this deer?"

And the boy pointed to the clearing. It did not take long for his mother to find the buck curled up in a nest of grasses. It watched them come close. Its antlers no longer looked majestic. The creature was too weak to hold its head high. Its eyes looked as faraway as the boy's. It moved its front legs a little, then gave up, resting its head on its back, licking its swollen wound.

"Just as I thought," the boy's mother said, eyeing its white spots. "Your deer." And she laid the boy beside the animal.

His mother collected wood and built a small fire and boiled water and threw in some herbs. She gave a cup to the deer, then a cup to the boy. She laid an herb-soaked cloth over the deer's wound and laid another one over the boy's. She fed her son and the buck the same food: fruits and berries and roasted mushrooms and boiled greens and nuts. She stroked her son's hair with one hand and the deer's fur with the other. She sang them songs in the language of humans and in the language of spirits.

The boy did not know how long he was there with his mother and the deer. Days? Weeks? Little by little, his world became clearer. Every time the boy opened his eyes, he saw the buck's eyes, looking into his. Its eyes grew bigger as the life came back into them. The boy felt as though he was looking into a mirror.

The boy smiled.

The deer smiled.

Then one morning, the boy woke up, and the deer's eyes were gone. Its spot in the grass was empty. The boy sat up and looked around, just in time to see the flash of a white tail disappearing into the trees.

The next day, the boy and his mother went home. For weeks he walked with a limp and a stick. Within months, he was running. And after a year passed, he was the fastest runner in his *pueblo* once again.

But it was different now. Now, every day, the boy ran along the edges of the deepest, most magical forest. He ran and felt his deer eyes watching the trees whiz by and felt his deer legs pounding the earth. He ran and ran, leaping over logs and fences. He became known as the protector of the forest. If anyone tried to enter, he would chase them, and always, he would catch them. People said that when he ran, a handsome buck with giant antlers bounded alongside him, just inside the forest's shadows. Together, they ran with their legs outstretched, the deer an echo of the boy, or maybe the boy an echo of the deer.

Years passed, and the boy became an old man, and still he ran along the forest, although more slowly now. Sometimes he stopped to rest and told his tale to the children who gathered around him. And always, Zitlally, he ended with this: "If you ever find yourself in the deepest, most magical forest, be kind to whatever creature you meet there. Look into its eyes. And smile."

A note about Immigration from Mexico to the U.S.A.

I was inspired to write *Star in the Forest* after hearing from a twelve-year-old reader who felt a connection with the main character, Clara, in my book *What the Moon Saw*. But this girl pointed out one big difference: Clara was born in the United States and could freely cross the Mexican border. This girl, however, had been born in Mexico and immigrated here illegally with her parents. They came to the United States to work because they couldn't find jobs in Mexico that would pay for decent housing, food, clothes, and education. This girl wanted to visit her relatives in Mexico, especially her father, who had recently been deported. But if she went, it would be too dangerous to return.

This girl's story is a common one in our country now, and part of a bigger immigration story. For hundreds of years, people—including my own ancestors—have moved here to find jobs and opportunities. But with every new wave of immigrants, Americans have faced challenges in adapting to the newcomers. Some Americans have worried that immigrants would change their lives for the worse. They have feared that newcomers would take their jobs, crowd their communities, bring crime, harm their values, unfairly use their resources, threaten their language, or damage their culture.

On the other hand, many Americans have focused on the good things that newcomers offer their communities. Thanks to immigration, the United States has a variety of music, languages, and foods that make people's lives richer. Newcomers often bring good family and work values, while paying taxes, spending money, and doing much-needed labor. Many Americans understand that immigrants are often escaping tough circumstances and doing their best to improve their families' lives.

During the late 1990s, I was living in a beautiful, but poor, region of Oaxaca, Mexico. Nearly everyone I knew had relatives in the United States, doing construction work, agricultural labor, hotel cleaning, and other physically demanding jobs. These people were undocumented immigrants because they were working in the United States without legal permission. My friends explained that while it was sad to have loved ones so far away, the money sent by their relatives paid for their families' basic needs.

After I moved from Mexico to the Southwest United States, I became friends with many Latin Americans who were undocumented immigrants. I've seen how their lives have changed as the government has more strictly enforced immigration laws in recent years. Previously, our country tolerated a certain level of illegal immigration because there were many physically demanding jobs that needed to be filled. In the early 2000s, however, the American government began to strengthen border security, punish companies that hired undocumented immigrants, and make it difficult for such immigrants to get a driver's license.

As a result, life has become very hard for my immigrant friends and their kids. Because they fear being deported to Mexico, bosses and coworkers can take advantage of them. Because they can't get a Colorado driver's license, they worry about the police pulling them over. And because of the tough security at the border, immigrants have to cross in more remote places, where they might be assaulted or kidnapped—both of which happened to a friend of mine. Now some immigrants feel too scared to return to Mexico for visits the way they used to. Other immigrants have decided to go back to Mexico permanently to live with their relatives, despite the poverty there. Other immigrants have been deported, often leaving kids and spouses behind in the United States.

This situation is especially hard for undocumented children. Many have spent their lives here, have gone to American schools, and speak English perfectly. They feel at home in the United States, but without legal papers, their opportunities for college and jobs are limited.

Right now, hardly anyone is happy with the state of undocumented immigration to the United States. Almost everyone agrees that the situation needs to change somehow; for example, through the creation of more migrant worker programs. Some people have proposed laws that would give undocumented immigrant teens legal status so that they can go to college and find professional jobs here. What do you think the solution is?

Please visit www.lauraresau.com for ideas on using this book to start a discussion of immigration issues.

Nahuatl* Glossary
and Pronunciation Guide

Ni-mitz nequi (*nee-MEETS nay-KEE*): I love you

Xono (*SHO-noh*): Zitlally's father's village

Zitlally (*seet-LAH-lee*): Star (spelling variation of *Citlali*)

*Nahuatl was the language of the ancient Aztecs. Forms of Nahuatl are still spoken by about one and a half million people. Most Nahuatl speakers come from rural communities in central Mexico, and their dialects often differ from village to village. Some English words derived from Nahuatl are *avocado*, *chili*, *chocolate*, *coyote*, and *tomato*. A number of Nahuatl names are now popular in Mexico, such as Xochitl (*SOH-cheel*; flower) and Cuauhtemoc (*coo-ow-TAY-mohc*; falling eagle).

Spanish Glossary
and Pronunciation Guide

bienvenido (*bee-AYN vay-NEE-doh*): welcome

deportado (*day-porr-TAH-doh*): deported

deportadas (*day-porr-TAH-dahs*): deported (feminine plural form)

el Norte (*ayl NOHRR-tay*): the North (refers to the United States)

estrella (*ays-TRAY-yah*): star

feliz cumpleaños (*fay-LEES coom-plee-AHN-yohs*): happy birthday

guapo (*GWAH-poh*): handsome

hasta mañana (*AHS-tah man-YAH-nah*): see you tomorrow

hermanas (*ayrr-MAH-nahs*): sisters

Jesús María José (*hay-ZOOS mah-REE-ah hoh-SAY*): Jesus Mary Joseph

la migra (*la MEE-grah*): border patrol

"Las Mañanitas" (*lahs mahn-yah-NEE-tahs*): a traditional birthday song

mi amor (*mee ah-MOHRR*): my love

migrantes (*mee-GRAHN-tays*): migrants

mi vida (*mee VEE-dah*): my life

m'hija (*MEE-hah*): my daughter

mucho gusto (*MOO-choh GOOS-toh*): nice to meet you

nervios (*NAYRR-vee-ohs*): nerves

noticias (*noh-TEE-see-ahs*): news

por favor (*porr fah-FOHRR*): please

pueblo (*PWAY-bloh*): town or village

que perro (*kay PAY-rroh*): what a dog

rancheras (*rrahn-CHAY-rahs*): kind of traditional Mexican music

se habla español (*say HAH-blah ays-pahn-YOHL*): Spanish spoken

secuestrado (*say-kways-TRAH-doh*): kidnapped

señora (*sayn-YOH-rah*): ma'am/Mrs.

señorita (*sayn-yoh-REE-tah*): miss/Ms.

si Dios quiere (*see dee-OHS kee-AY-ray*): God willing

suelo (*SWAY-loh*): [hit the] ground

telenovelas (*tay-lay-noh-VAY-lahs*): soap operas

tres leches (*TRAYS LAY-chays*): three milks (a kind of cake)

vámonos (*VAH-moh-nohs*): let's go

About the Author

Laura Resau lived in the Mixtec region of Oaxaca, Mexico, for two years as an English teacher and anthropologist. After teaching English to immigrants in the southwest United States for nearly a decade, she now writes full-time in Colorado, where she lives with her husband, her dog, and her son. She is also the author of *What the Moon Saw* and *Red Glass*.